Grayson,
   You are a lucky little lady to be blessed with your gift. Can't wait to see all of the good you will do for the world with it. - Love
Asad

Isabelle Brave
Written and illustrated by:
Evelyn Kennedy

A note for adult readers:

The intention of this book is to empower intuitive, empathic, and highly sensitive children to utilize their own energetic and emotional protection mechanisms.

Many children feel defenseless against draining entities and will benefit from the practices described in the following pages. All of the examples used in the book are just a starting point for how these systems can be put in place by children. As their grown-ups, we can teach them to trust their intuition in creating the best system for them just like Isabelle Brave.

You will notice in this book there are no gender assignments for characters or assumptions made about familial living environments. This is intentional to provide flexibility for your own dynamic and to represent the diverse ways we all experience family.

As protection energy is secular, this book does not project any specific affiliations with organized religion, but feel free to insert the use of any spiritual guides that are impactful to your family, religion or culture.

Out of celebration and respect of neuro-diversity, the fonts and formatting used in this book are designed to support dyslexic readers.

You will find a guided meditation in the back of this book to assist you in taking the child (or yourself!) through the steps of clearing their energy field, building their own bubble and bringing in allies for support.

My name is Isabelle Brave...
                    but I am scared.

I feel every bump in the night, I get cold and clammy, my heart races, and my body shakes inside while my outsides are still.

I see shadows and ghosts
and creepies in the windows.

Sometimes I feel like they are reaching out for me, so I run into my grown-ups room.

They'll say I just have nighmares, or an active imagination, (whatever that means). But I know what I am up against.
I know what I have to do.

I will take a deeeeeep breath. I will expand my body until I am feeling very big and powerful.

I will use my brain to build a bubble around me.

Everyday I change my bubble, sometimes it's pink, sometimes it's green, sometimes it's soft, and sometimes it's shiny. Sometimes it's shaped like a pyramid, or a crystal, and sometimes I need to bring a friend in with me!

In my bubble I bring my stuffed animals, a strong warrior friend and a slimy snail. I feel a gentle breeze, I sit on some squishy moss. Sometimes I bring someone I miss. There are times when I feel like I need a WHOLE TEAM of helpers in my bubble with me!

The next time I feel the yucky feelings, I build my bubble with my thoughts and my breath, I summon my helpers. With all of them around me I feel brave and strong. This time when I know the creepies are near, my team knows what to do.

We tell the creepies they cannot come inside my bubble. If we want to we can send them healing light. We can help their hurts if they want to feel better, and then send them on their way.

AND IT WORKS!
I am protected by my guides, friends and allies in my bubble. The creepies know I am untouchable.

The more I play with my friends in my bubble, the more I know they are always here to support me when I call on them! I feel safe and strong.

My name is Isabelle Brave...
and I am powerful and peaceful in my body

...and rested.

A Guided Meditation to share with your child:

Take 5 deep breaths. As you take the air into your lungs feel your chest getting bigger and bigger and more full. Let's count your breaths together, 1, 2, 3, 4, 5. Now let's inflate your bubble. Notice what color your bubble is. Is it round? Or a different shape? Can you see through your bubble? Notice whats it's made of. How do you feel in your bubble? Look around your creation and notice if there's anything you need to adjust about your space. Is there anything there that you want to remove? Anything you want to be here with you? Now let's call in some helpers to your bubble! Who do you feel would be a powerful friend to have with you today? Think of what you need to feel the most cozy, comfortable and light. Let's ask your friends to bring in everything you need! Remember that the only things welcome in your bubble are things you invite in, nothing can bother you here. You are safe and held. You are safe and held. You are safe and held.

You can stay in your bubble as long as you like, or you can choose to bring it everywhere with you.

About the Author

Evelyn Kennedy is a lifelong intuitive. She began honing her skills after the birth of her daughter Daphne (the inspiration for this book) in 2013. With an innate understanding of the scary parts of her abilities from childhood, Evelyn knew she wanted to provide context to her daughter and other empathic and sensitive kids and offer support and empowerment to parents that might not have access to the same tools.

She is a Washington native and lives with her two children Daphne and Cosmo, her partner Jess, and her father Will. She loves creating in all mediums and considers herself an artist and teacher. Evelyn offers a variety of classes for self improvement as well as energetic tools available at www.themirrorgrid.com.

For my Daphne Lou

CPSIA information can be obtained
at www.ICGtesting.com
Printed in the USA
BVHW021109191220
595975BV00002B/19

9 781087 930923